the DOT

Aaruni Khan

ISBN 979-8-88629-986-1

Disclaimer

NEW YORK, USA

1

The Manhattan skyline is famous for its picturesque views, especially at daybreak, when soft rays of the morning sun reflect on tall glass and steel structures that stood magnificently along the embankment on the other side. An image of it on the translucent water of Hudson makes the scenery a photographic pleasure.

Bob, a natural scientist, lived in Hoboken, in New Jersey, and was content with the carefree life since his retirement. He enjoyed traveling to faraway places and had been an itinerant to exotic locations, especially in Africa and Southeast Asia. As part of his fitness regime, Bob was a habitual morning walker; and been walking along the riverside every day while savoring the view that always mesmerized him while observing the perfection of nature's beauty that splendidly blended with the architectural grandeur of the city that never sleeps. With the brightening of the sun, he resumes walking along his usual path, waving and wishing to fellow walkers, though he never knew their names.

On November 1st, Bob came back from his walk and settled down on his favorite couch. It faced a balcony that overlooked a children's park, which was mostly deserted during the morning hours as the kids were either at school or left at the crèche by their working parents. He poured First Flush Darjeeling tea, his favorite morning beverage, in a cup from the teapot mounted on a warmer by his side, which he habitually keeps ready before leaving home for the early morning stroll. While sipping tea, he felt the weather was warming up and pulled down the blinds to get some respite from the heat that radiated through the windows.

2

*B*ob finished the morning chores and sat down for breakfast. He was not in a hurry, as he had no plans for going out in that scorching weather. The Met Office had forecasted that similar weather would continue for a few more days, even though it was not normal around that time of the year when Thanksgiving was just weeks away.

He finished breakfast, cleared the table, took a cup of coffee, and lit a cigarette. Leisurely he started flipping through the newspaper, though mostly filled with trivial news and advertisements. His interest was in news articles on global warming and adverse climate changes, even though they were about topics already discussed at previously held climate conferences. Nevertheless, a particular headline on that day rang the alarm bell and aroused his curiosity. The headline on the front page was **"2015 -2021, on-track to be hottest on record."**

The news stated that according to United Nations statistics, a mere rise of 2 degrees Celsius in global temperatures above pre-industrialization levels would be catastrophic. The World Meteorological Office report also confirmed that average global temperatures had already exceeded more than 50% of the estimated threshold. The extant rise of 1.09 degrees Celsius had caused extreme weather events around the world like flash-floods, drought, melting of glaciers, rising sea levels, and intermittent cyclones and tornadoes. The impact was experienced everywhere, from the mountain tops to the depths of the sea.

All the state leaders, environmental scientists, and climate champions were having brainstorming sessions throughout successive Climate Conferences to find a solution without much progress thus far. However, the consensus had been that industrialization and incremental usage of fossil fuels should be blamed for rising temperatures, which primarily took place over the last 200 years. Although, greenhouse gas emissions existed historically, albeit at varying degrees.

While slowly releasing smoke, engrossed in the thought of global warming, he realized that the warning bell had already rung, and the world was not very far from the day when all living organisms would feel the brunt on their livelihoods. Bob found it very upsetting, but at the same time could not reconcile his mind with the concept of industrialization and the usage of fossil fuels as the rationale for such an unprecedented situation.

His mind continued searching for some logical explanation that would support the hypothesis. Industries and those using fossil fuels are not the only emitters *of greenhouse gases. There are nearly eight billion people on earth and by far many more species of other living organisms who also release carbon dioxide while breathing 24/7/365 throughout their lives. It took the world's population only about 200 years to reach a figure of nearly eight billion from just about one billion, putting enormous pressure on available natural resources, which also roughly coincided with the industrialization phase.*

Progress in medical science has also contributed to population growth by extending the life expectancy of humans by about ten years in the last one hundred years, combined with a significant reduction in the infant mortality rate. The cumulative effect of population growth and consequent industrial expansion had led to deforestation of large chunks and environmental pollution. Another collateral impact of deforestation had been the displacement of wildlife, which facilitated zoonosis (transmission of muted viruses from animals to humans) that led to a worldwide pandemic of diseases in addition to other catastrophic climate events.

All of the above logic wasn't enough to clarify the doubts that Bob had in mind and to justify the rise in global temperatures because there had been a slow but consistent increase in temperatures worldwide, even before the industrialization phase that stretched over the last 200 years. The world community had ignored that fact due to the unavailability of reliable data, which could have facilitated realistic estimations.

He did some research to find the current scenario. Read all the available news articles and research papers in the public domain, though he could not make much headway as they depicted only the effects of climate change but not the actual cause.

Finally, he summarized his understanding and concluded that the unrestricted growth in population, industrial expansion, widespread deforestation, and resultant environmental pollution were the consequences of irresponsible human behavior that resulted from their incoherent and negligent attitude. Hence, people on earth are squarely responsible for creating a situation where there is no way out.

3

*B*ob poured some more coffee from the percolator and with the coffee cup in hand, drifted back to the topic of climate change. He was so engrossed with the deliberations that he added more carbon dioxide into the atmosphere by lighting a few more cigarettes.

His mind was working hard on global warming when a phone call from Willy brought him back to reality. Willy was one of his few friends who had called him over to invite for dinner that evening at Jason's Court on Newark Street. He requested Bob to be there around 5:30 pm to discuss an important topic, and Bob, not having any particular plan, accepted it, hoping to have a good time with Willy that evening.

Bob drove his black Audi e-Tron, and in about 15 minutes, reached Jason's Court. He found Willy waiting near the entrance while parking his car. They touched their elbows, observing the COVID19 protocol. While entering, Willy informed that a corner table had been booked for them, which was away from the music, so that they could talk peacefully and also enjoy the food, for which the place was quite famous.

They went inside together, and the waiter, by the name of Martha, guided them to the designated table in the right-hand corner, which was hardly visible from the remaining restaurant. She took the orders and left after tucking a slip of paper in a long multi-colored glass at the center of the table. Bob thought that she looked prettier when she smiled because of her pearly teeth. She should be in her mid-thirties and had the figure of an athlete.

They settled down on either side of the table, facing each other. Willy stared at him intently for some time, as if he was trying to read Bob's mind, expecting some questions inquiring the reasons for the unplanned dinner invite at such short notice. Bob was also quite eager to know about the matter for which he was invited there and silently signaled to continue while expecting him to seek his advice on some complex deal, as Willy knew his strengths.

Martha placed the drinks on the table along with a platter full of tacos for munching until they decided on the food from the dinner menu. They raised their wine glasses and cheered, wishing good health for the entire world in the COVID-19-induced pandemic situation.

After taking a long sip, Willy broke the silence by telling Bob that he would discuss an important topic, and the confidentiality of which was of paramount importance. In the age of the open internet and widespread hacking, one should be careful with confidential matters, and that's the reason for meeting Bob in person. He was sure that they were being tracked and under constant vigil, even right at that moment within the restaurant. But as long as they communicated in person, the conversation would remain confidential. He also told Bob that he had reached the place before him and did a bug-check to ensure secrecy of their discussion. Bob was astonished to learn about his style of operation, although he knew that Willy was involved in lots of secret deals, which made him further impatient to hear all about whatever he wanted to discuss.

Before raising the topic, Willy talked about a deal that he had done with a powerful and influential person, who had agents in some important countries, spread over almost all the continents including, the United States; And continued narrating an intriguing brief of what he had intended to say. Bob found the entire mission quite exhilarating, while his scientific brain started working hard to equate what Willy had said and his understanding for having a pragmatic view of it.

Dinner was over. Willy asked for the check from Martha and told Bob that he had planned a trip to the Maldives; an archipelagic nation located in the middle of the Indian Ocean and is about 750 miles southwest of Sri Lanka. He wanted Bob to accompany him as his knowledge would add lots of value to their mission, though further details would unfold in phases after reaching the Maldives.

Finally, Bob understood the purpose of the meeting and where his fitment would be in the bigger picture. He *appreciated Willy for taking him into confidence and conveyed thanks for inviting him on a trip to the Maldives. Bob's passion was traveling, especially to faraway places like the Maldives. It was an unvisited destination, so he welcomed the pleasant surprise by agreeing to be on board.*

Willy, standing up for leaving around half-past nine, told Bob that it would be a simple travel plan for them as tourists and the details of it would reach him by email the following day.

4

Back home, Bob watched TV news briefly and retired for the day. While in bed, he thought about the secret mission that Willy had shared and made a few mental notes for action the following day.

After the usual morning routine, Bob sat down to check emails. He usually stayed away from it to avoid the irritation of seeing the primary inbox full of junk. That day was different. He looked at the inbox and was happy to find an email from Willy's travel agent, only the third from the top. Bob knew him as an organized person, and as expected, all the booking confirmations were there for their trip to the Maldives by Emirates Airways, with a layover in Dubai.

The journey was on November 07th, only four days away, and Bob was elated as his wait would be over soon in getting an opportunity to explore a new place. Instantly, he thanked Willy by the return email and started jotting down important action points on his "Things to Do" list.

Before anything else, the thought of Diana came to his mind. Although they lived in two different locations, *she had been his life's motivation right through. He immediately called up Diana to inform her about the trip to the Maldives and promised to visit her on returning from Asia.*

5

As part of secrecy, Bob had agreed during the meeting at Jason's Court that they would meet again, only at the Airport on the travel date.

The next few days, Bob was busy shopping for essentials that he might need during his travel and stay in the Maldives. He also made some manual notes in a pocket-size notepad from his leather-covered fat notebook, usually kept with other documents, inside a locker hidden behind a large painting on a wall inside his library. In between, he had also visited the Hoboken Historical Museum to take note of some reference points.

On November 7th, Bob got ready early and ticked off all the boxes on his checklist after verifying them so that nothing was left behind.

The flight to the Maldives was at 10:40 hours by Emirates Airways from JFK, New York. There was a layover in Dubai for 18 hours and 35 minutes and, would be arriving at Velana International Airport near Male, the capital of Maldives, was on November 9th at 07:40 hours, local time.

Bob, in casual attire, reached the Airport around 7:30 am and found Willy, already there, waiting for him at the Business Lounge. He completed self-service check-in formalities and dropped off the luggage at the Airline counter before joining Willy for breakfast. Usually, Bob was a light traveler, but for the trip to the Maldives, he had packed more stuff, as a buffer, in case their stay got extended.

They finished breakfast, and before boarding the plane, they smoked their last cigarettes inside the smoking zone. Presently, loudspeaker announcements have been stopped in airports to reduce sound pollution. Willy checked the flight status, which showed that boarding had already started. Both of them quickly proceeded to the boarding gate and into the aircraft.

A beautiful Russian Air-hostess, dressed in her official uniform, greeted them on board and assisted in stowing their hand luggage in the overhead luggage compartment. Willy had booked twin business class seats in the first row along the right-hand window-side to get some extra leg space for them as it was a long haul with a flying time of more than 12 hours.

After settling down on their seats, they wiped and sanitized their hands with wet towels. The host served welcome drinks and chocolates while the refueling of the aircraft was going on. Willy pulled out a tourist guidebook on the Maldives from a folder and passed it on to Bob, telling him that it had some information that might be handy. He also talked about sharing additional details on their mission after reaching the island resort, near a place called **Dharavandhoo,** *in the Maldives.*

The aircraft was a new bird, absolutely clean and sanitized as per COVID19 protocol. The funny part was that it was difficult to make out who was seated next as everyone was wearing masks completely covering their nose and mouth. Some were wearing double masks and also head caps. Bob thought with dismay, how long such an abnormal, which some say a "New Normal" situation would continue; God only knew.

The team leader of the crew announced the completion of boarding and closure of all the doors. The plane started rolling at the scheduled departure time, taxiing through the runway while picking up speed for take-off. Bob inserted the booklet inside the seat pocket and switched on the personalized display screen to check whether anything worth watching was there but dozed off sooner than he realized.

6

*T*he window shutters were down to avoid the glaring sun that appeared to be moving alongside, and most of the fellow passengers were in slumber. He could hear some whispers, but hardly one could make out what they were talking about or in which language. A couple of air-hosts hurriedly passed Bob, appearing a bit worried, went towards the cockpit from the tail-end.*

Bob suddenly felt the urge to look through the window, bypassing Willy, who occupied the window seat. At first, he thought the plane was flying over the sea before approaching the airport as it was flying pretty low. His eyes searched for more than 30 minutes to view the airstrip but could see nothing other than seawater. To share the discomfort, he pushed Willy and asked him to take a look.

Willy woke up from sleep and looked outside through the window and at the front monitor that showed the travel route and distance covered. It was blank. He quickly got up from his seat and went towards the crew station next to the cockpit door. He came back in 2 minutes with a horrified look that Bob had never seen before. In a hoarse voice, he told Bob that the plane had lost connection with the Air Traffic Control, and the last news they had was that entire Middle-East Asia got submerged due to a sudden rise in sea levels, for reasons not known.

It took a while for them to apprehend the situation and realize the severity of the crisis. The plane could not land anywhere as there was no land visible within sight and unable to re-establish contact with the Air Traffic Controls for seeking their guidance. Willy got up again and went inside the cockpit to speak to the pilots. They informed him that their only hope was to fly at a low altitude towards the north and forcefully land at an operational airport in the vicinity.

They were at the last leg of the flight, and the fuel tank was near empty, which further aggravated the crisis and gravity of the situation. However, if all were lucky on board, still the chances of survival were quite bleak. The captain had instructed the crew not to announce anything at that stage to avoid any panicky situation among passengers. Had the information been given, it would have made things worse for them to manage the trial to ensure the survival of 269 passengers on board. Bob thought that only Willy had his ways of extracting information at difficult times.

Suddenly Bob felt like a jerk and woke up realizing that it was a horrifying dream. All was well, and a sumptuous lunch was about to be served. The host was there to note down his choice of food, dessert, and accompanying drinks. He ordered chicken breast with boiled vegetables, spinach, olives, and a platter of assorted cheese followed by Brazilian black coffee so that he wouldn't doze off again.

7

A sip of Brazilian black coffee activated Bob's nerves. His brain started working on the subject, which was the real reason for their travel. He took out the guidebook on the Maldives from the seat pocket and started flipping through pages looking for some relevant information that might be helpful during their stay in the island country.

Bob knew that they were going to land at Velana International Airport, which is on Hulhule Island adjacent to Male, the capital of Maldives. It is an archipelagic nation comprising 1192 coral islands grouped in a double chain of 26 atolls that stretch along 871 kilometers north to south and 130 kilometers east to west. The total dry land area is 298 square kilometers only. It is the lowest country, having average ground levels of only 1.5 meters (4.11 ft) above sea levels. More than 80% of the country's land area comprises coral islands, which rise only 1 meter from sea levels. As a result, Maldivian Islands are at a very high risk of getting destroyed by submerging due to rising sea levels at the current levels of global warming, resulting from rapid climate change across the world.

The Maldives had experienced the indication of such a natural phenomenon at the time of the Tsunami on December 24th, 2004. It was a result of an underwater earthquake in the Indian Ocean. The country was devastated. Out of 1192 islands, only nine had escaped flooding. Fourteen islands had to be vacated, while six of them got destroyed. According to researchers from the University of Southampton, Maldives is one of the most endangered Island Nations under present circumstances.

In the Maldives, being archipelagic, internal travel is quite different from other places and primarily comprises ATR 72-600 aircraft and DHC-6 Twin Otter Seaplanes. Additionally, there are speed boats and indigenous motorized boats called "Dhoni." Bob found the information quite handy. The place had different characteristics, which made it pretty interesting.

Tourism being the second most important industry after fishing, there are exotic beach resorts and are well-equipped with all the western comforts. Bob tried visualizing the islands surrounded by aquamarine water, bathed in bright sunlight and the tropical weather. Instantly he decided to stay long enough to cover most of the islands there and would use seaplanes for movement. It was quite possible that many of the islands may not exist by the end of this decade and would never get a chance to visit them. He immediately broached the idea with Willy, who agreed, but only after completing their mission. They continued discussing how the Maldives is different from any other place. It was invaded several times and finally became an Islamic state imposing severe restrictions on women, not adhering to any Human Rights guidelines. Tourism, being a cash cow and contributing handsomely to their GDP, none of the limitations apply to foreigners.

A soft announcement came through overhead speakers, requesting passengers to fasten their seatbelts, straighten their backrests, and so on. The flight was about to land in Dubai shortly. As the flight descended, the beautifully planned city of Dubai was coming into sight. Bob remembered his dream and felt much relieved.

DUBAI, UAE

8

*B*ob had visited Dubai quite often and had been familiar with the city. It was more than 18 hours of layover. The passengers heading to the Maldives were accommodated in the Hotel Marriott by Emirates Airways. The airline staff guided them, along with other passengers, through the terminal and directed them to designated cars for dropping off at the hotel. Bob appreciated the hospitality extended by the airline and the hotel.

After taking a rest for a while, he freshened up and dialed Willy's room number to inform him that he would be waiting in the hotel lobby. It was expansive and brightly illuminated, arranged with comfortable seating arrangements, well-spaced out for different group sizes. Bob sat down on one of the two single couches facing the elevator bay to see Willy coming. The lady at the travel desk near the entrance was busy talking to a young couple, who appeared to be from East Asia. A group seated at a distance looked like having a serious discussion. Bob looked around to find out if smoking was permitted but could not find anyone smoking. He decided to glance *through the newspaper and, while taking it from the low height table in the front, noticed the ashtray and a matchbox. It indicated that it was a smoking zone and lit a cigarette. He wondered what plan Willy would be having during their stay in Dubai and saw him coming out of the elevator, looking for Bob.*

The weather in Dubai was reasonably comfortable, but Willy preferred staying in the hotel as that break was quite relaxing after being confined inside the aircraft for nearly fourteen hours since they boarded at JFK Airport. Again, as they were traveling against the clock, the break would help tide them over jet lag when they would reach the Maldives the next day.

They had breakfast at the hotel around half-past ten and felt sleepy. It was their bedtime in the US, and their body clock functioned as per the US clock. They went back to their rooms on the 5th floor and crashed on the bed to catch up on their sleep. They would be having hardly any time to sleep at night as the next leg of the flight from Dubai was at 4.30 in the morning. The travel desk informed them that transport from the airline would be there for pick-up at 2.00 am sharp, and the concierge at the Bell-desk would collect the luggage for loading in the cars at 01.45 am.

Bob and Willy slept throughout the day apart from waking up to have their meals. There was no need for sightseeing or shopping as they were transiting through Dubai and had been familiar with the place.

At the scheduled time, they proceeded to the airport. The flight was on time, and the flight duration from Dubai to the Maldives was about four and a half hours. The expected time to reach Velana International Airport was around 09:30 am, UAE time, and 7.40 am, local time in the Maldives.

They settled down in their respective seats, and by the time the plane took off the ground, both of them had dozed off. They woke up around eight and had breakfast. Strong black coffee was served after breakfast, as chosen by them, to get out of their sleepy mode.

MALDIVES

9

In a short while, the flight started its descent and landed at Velana International Airport about 10 minutes before the scheduled arrival time. In contrast to Dubai Airport, it was much smaller. Though, the tourist assistance was quite impressive. The immigrations were pretty fast as Americans enjoyed visa exemptions. They collected their luggage and stood in the queue for transit passengers. They had another short internal flight that would take them to Dharavandhoo, where Willy had booked one of the exclusive resorts entirely for them and a few other guests, who would arrive during the day from different parts of the world.

The flight to Dharavandhoo was by an ATR Airplane, and the experience was quite similar to taking a bus service in a third-world country. The aircraft was full of local people carrying loads of hand luggage, mostly stuffed under their seats. The flight was for about 40 minutes. A car from the resort picked them up from the airport, and they reached there around 10:00 am.

The resort was on the ocean, in a jutted-out part of an island. It was connected to the mainland by a narrow strip, just wide enough to accommodate the passing of two cars. It was nestled within densely planted coconut trees and had an opening towards the beach, and the whole landscape was pictorial. The height of the hard soil was just about one meter above sea level, which gave a feeling that the resort was almost floating on water in the middle of the Indian Ocean from where no other landmass was visible in any direction.

Bob thought it to be a perfect selection for the type of discussion they would be having, ensuring the required level of confidentiality. He appreciated Willy for his thoughtfulness and organizing skills. There were eight huts; built on elevated platforms of about 6 feet in height. It had a traditional look, with ladder-like stairs for climbing to the exclusive balconies that encircled the rooms with sitting arrangements made of bamboo. But inside the hut-like room, it was strikingly modern, with mostly all the amenities of the western world. It was a very thoughtful blend of tradition with modernity. Bob and Willy were very excited as they had never experienced living in such an exclusive and exotic environment.

A young, well-built man with a finely manicured beard and traditional attire took the luggage into the respective rooms. All the rooms had a view of the ocean through the tinted glass windows. There was a nice breeze outside. However, air-conditioning in the room was a definite need. The manager of the resort, accompanied by a bearer carrying drinks in two slender glasses, came forward to introduce himself and mentioned his name as

Hamid. He offered drinks made of coconut water as a part of their traditional way of welcoming guests.

While having the drink, Willy checked with Hamid about the other guests who were expected during the day and was happy to know that everything was on schedule. He gave instructions to Hamid for setting up a casual sitting arrangement for six people under colorful umbrellas near the beach, and for a dedicated person to take orders from them. While going in for a shower and freshening up, Bob ordered some snacks made from a local recipe and chilled beer for them when they would be back at the beach camp.

10

*B*ob started feeling restless as he had no clue about anything beyond that point. He decided to bring up the topic with Willy to get a heads-up on the way forward before the scene got formal with the presence of others who would be arriving around lunchtime.

Bob, formally known as Robert Quest,wassix feet tall with a well-built physique. He had celebrated his 62nd birthday a couple of months back, although he looked much younger than his age. His tanned complexion, cleanly shaven face and a pair of thin-rimmed glasses gave him an intelligent look. He was generally serious-natured but occasionally cracked jokes with his friends whenever his mind was relatively free.

By profession, Bob was a Natural Scientist. His specialization was in Earth and Space Science. It is a branch of science concerning the description, understanding, and prediction of natural phenomena, based on empirical evidence from observation and experimentation. Its subdivisions are physical science, earth & space science, and life science. It's the science that deals with matter, energy and their interrelations *and transformations, or the objectively measurable phenomena. Bob had been researching the principles of Galileo until the time of opting for severance from his tenured job but kept himself updated with natural events that occurred around the world. His mind was busy with different thoughts since he met Willy at Jason's Court in New Jersey. Enough time had elapsed since then and, it was high time to have clarity on the proposed mission.*

Bob got ready for an informal day wearing khaki shorts, a Black Tee-shirt, and a pair of sneakers, which gave the impression of an informal gathering rather than a meeting of experts from different countries. Before going out of the room, he called up Diana and informed his safe arrival. He gave a brief description of the place, especially the exclusivity of the resort, and his experience of standing at the edge of a tiny island in the middle of the Indian Ocean, enjoying the beauty of the coral reef. Bob captured the beauty of nature on his cell phone and sent a few pictures to Diana with a short text. He felt a bit relieved as his cell phone was getting signals and would keep him connected to the rest of the world.

Diana Walsh *has been a well-known name in the financial world and a familiar face among regular television viewers, owing to her frequent appearances as an expert for talks with media people. At times, Bob watched her talk to the TV host and other corporate personalities and appreciated her elegance and wittiness. Diana had always been busy managing her own consulting business. Mostly* *she was occupied on the phone to discuss strategies and plans with her clients and business associates.*

*Bob came out in the open and found Willy was conversation with a middle-aged person who appeared to be of Chinese origin. On coming closer, Willy introduced him to the newcomer as **Mr. Sung Wen**, who was about five feet and five inches tall, well-built, and a cleanly shaved man around 50 years old. Both of them looked straight into their eyes and shook hands while Bob introduced himself. Mr. Wen had just arrived from Singapore, excused himself, and proceeded to the allotted room to get refreshed.*

Bob pulled up a chair to sit beside Willy and asked him about the way forward and his expectations from all the experts.

Willy took a long drag from his cigarette and started by referring to the news about leaders of the forty-five participating countries and their pledge to take all possible measures within their powers and in their respective countries. It is to reduce the release of greenhouse gas and thereby restrain the extent of global warming within the agreed limit of 1.5 Degrees Celsius above the average temperature that prevailed before the industrial revolution or the time from where civilization had already moved ahead by more than 150 years.

In that context, the Global Committee had contemplated a host of restrictive measures to be implemented over the next few decades. Primarily in less developed nations around the world, to save humanity from the impact of adverse climatic events that had resulted from the rise in global temperatures. The budget for such expenditures had been agreed at US$100 billion annually. It was a top-line declaration, with lots of fanfare, by the global leaders of a few rich nations. However, the ground-level situation is different in each of the pledging countries. The social, economic, and infrastructural disparities would raise diverse and unique issues, which political leaders would find difficult to solve, resulting in a lack of intent in acting. These actions have been agreed upon on paper without any legal binding. Hence, the conferences of parties would turn out to be an annual ritual like the previous conferences especially, when the actual results of perceived actions; would be known decades later. Also, it is quite possible that in most nations, many present leaders would either not be alive or may not be in power. Most importantly, there are possibilities that the onus of these farfetched goals may not get the attention of future leadership when priorities are changing very fast in this dynamic world.

Willy paused momentarily and looked at Bob, expecting some comments, but Bob remained silent, signaling him to continue. Willy lit another cigarette and continued saying that whatever he had said were all published news, and the entire world knew about it. Then the question was why all the Global leaders were so concerned, trying to save humanity for the forthcoming generations, without knowing how life on earth would *be in the next millennium. That's because a sizable population, who are dedicated climate activists and are seriously concerned about the existence of humanity, is creating lots of noise to draw the attention of global leaders.*

Presently, activists, scientists, and leaders have no clue about the cause of the consistent rise in temperatures. And no one is willing to admit this fact to the world population. The effect of rising atmospheric temperatures is known and accepted without knowing the actual cause. The purpose of their meeting at the Maldives, involving some of the most knowledgeable scientists from different fields of science, was to establish a conclusive theory that would facilitate finding the most sought-after cause of Global Warming and the consequences of the resultant climatic changes.

11

*W*hile Willy continued, Bob drifted to the days when he was engaged in exploring planetary movements concerning the laws of nature. Bob's research was about the cycle of planetary birth and death, which had originated from a Dot, a point that could signify the beginning and also the end. It was a point of exploding desire whence came the Universe into existence and the cycle of Birth and Death completed. It's the same Dot that subsumes the entire creation. The explosion of the Dot, which gave birth to the Universe, was portrayed in the Big Bang Theory. Once the Universe ceases to expand and begins to contract, it will again go to its Dot form, only to be reborn once again.

It took millions of years for a chunk of molten liquid, supposed to have been spun off from the sun, to cool down while taking on the spherical shape because of high-speed rotation and as it traveled much further away from its present position. The powerful pull from the sun restricted the planet from moving away from it any further. The inertia of motion continued and formed an elliptical path, and the newly formed unidentified body started to revolve around the sun in its orbit continually. The speed of its *rotation and revolution started slowing down and evolved as a new planet, segregating solids from the liquid to form land and water. The growth of vegetation on it made the platform ready for living organisms, which started with the birth of a single cell amoeba.*

As per the laws of the Universe, as growth stops, the planet Earth will follow a reversal process of decay, disintegration, and extinction or death over millions of years to disappear from its orbit or path, making space for a new planet.

Bob had visualized the entire life cycle of the earth in his mind several times and was sure that it would move in that direction over a very long timescale spread over millions of years. No power on earth could do anything to overrule destiny. He compared his plight to that of the famous physicist and philosopher Galileo Di Vincenzo Bonaiuti de' Galilei. During Galileo's time, no one had ever believed his theory of Copernican Heliocentrism or the concept of the "Earth rotating daily and also revolving the Sun." This universal truth took a long time for people to understand and believe.

12

William Murray, or Willy, was a practical man. He had been busy trying to widen his network of powerful and influential people in business or politics so that he could strike high-value deals for his clients against a handsome fee for himself. He believed only in the present and how he could derive benefits for his clients and self. The meeting on the Maldivian Islands was arranged with a similar intent, as he had struck a deal with a very high profile, influential, and powerful person by putting his neck under a guillotine. Willy and his secret client were the only people who knew the real purpose of the meeting, along with renowned scientists from nations across the globe.

Willy checked with Hamid and was happy to note that all the invitees had arrived and they were available for the introductory meeting that evening. Bob and Willy went back to their rooms after finishing lunch. Bob had been introduced to Dr. Wen briefly and would get to know others in the evening. Before the meeting, he wanted to refer to the notes he had made from his notebook to organize his thoughts for articulating his theory to the elite group in a more credible manner.

At 6.00 pm, Bob came out of his room and headed towards the open-to-sky meeting venue on the beach. He ordered a cup of strong black coffee to clear his mind and energize his nerves. While settling down on a reclining chair, he appreciated the beauty of nature at sunset. The island was very strategically situated, as both the view of sunrise and sunsets were astounding. The reflection of the pale evening sun on dark blue water painted the surface crimson while portraying the partially sinking sun at the horizon. The continuous breaking of waves against the coastline reminded him of the process of relentless creation and destruction.

Willy, looking complacent, joined Bob with a cup of coffee held in his right hand and a cigarette between his lips. He informed him that all the other guests were to join them in a little while. He briefed Bob that he would set up the stage with an introduction session, followed by each of the guests putting forth their perspective on the subject, and Bob would be the concluding speaker of the day.

Willy also informed him that he had done some fact-checking on Bob's research. And that was the reason for getting him to the Maldives. Before Bob could say anything, Willy went ahead to welcome and greet the esteemed guests.

Willy started by introducing himself and Bob to the group, followed by the three gentlemen and a lady beginning with **Dr. Sung Wen,** *who had come from*

Singapore, was a Natural Scientist by profession and had specialized in Earth and Space science. He had arrived in the morning and was introduced to Bob briefly.

The next gentleman was **Dr. Eric Brown,** who had come from Bournemouth in Southern **UK**. He was about six feet tall, cleanly shaved, with dark brown hair brushed backward. His thin lips, wide-forehead, and a pair of black-framed spectacles gave him an accomplished look.

Then **Dr. Chang Min** introduced himself. He was an Astrophysicist, had come from **Tokyo,** and had a distinctive Japanese look, having thick black hair, cleanly shaved, and a smiling face. He wore a pair of rimless glasses.

Finally, the only lady in the group introduced herself as **Dr. Elena Nikolova** coming from **Moscow**. She was a heavyset person of about five feet and eight inches in height, having short light-brown hair and a whitish complexion. Her specialization was in Cosmology, and she had been working for the Soviet Space program.

13

*F*ive *gentlemen and a lady sat around the table with curious faces, except Dr. Chang Min, and had a brief conversation while the drinks and snacks were getting ready. It took nearly 10 minutes for the attendant to serve. They raised their glasses in unison and cheered for the success of their meeting and the safety of humanity.*

Willy, taking a sip from his drink, stood up; and with the consent of all the guests, addressed the group with a welcome note and thanked them for accepting his request at such short notice. He also explained the reasons for selecting the Maldives as the venue for their meeting. It was primarily for two reasons. Firstly, it's purely a tourist destination and would not raise any suspicion among other interested parties. The second point was more important, as it is the lowest landmass, from sea level, and is supposed to be one of the most endangered places in the world. Therefore, it was undoubtedly, the ideal place for uncovering the truth and establishing the theory for saving humanity.

Willy continued with the news of a pledge, as was taken by 45 countries, to save life on earth. They have imposed restrictions on the usage of fossil fuels. Especially in less developed countries, to control the rise in global atmospheric temperatures within the limit of 1.5 degrees Celsius above the estimated average temperature that had prevailed during the pre-industrialization period, which was approximately about two hundred years back in history. Again, the earth's tilt determines the amount of radiation received at a particular location. Therefore, the averaging out of the temperatures between the highest and the lowest points didn't make much logical sense; the reason being that the impact of adverse climatic events would not be the same at all the places and would deflect attention from where it is needed more.

The economic analysis had shown how global warming, which had already taken place, impacted livelihoods in different countries. The cumulative effects of global warming have hurt the GDP of many counties. Experts have estimated that if atmospheric temperatures rose above 2.0 degrees Celsius, the result would be catastrophic; the projected timeline for such a catastrophe to happen is around 2050, which is only about three decades away.

*It also appeared from statements by global leaders that all these estimates were not worthy of trust, as they already knew the real threat that was looming in the backyard. At the 26th Conference of Parties, the British Prime Minister had expressed the truth clearly by saying to the world that "**It's one minute to midnight on the Doomsday Clock**"and that it was not contradicted or* *opposed by any global leader or the scientific fraternity. At that point, Willy requested Dr. Eric Brown to elaborate on the statement made by the Prime Minister of his country at the Global Conference, held in Glasgow, and share his perspective on global warming and climatic changes with others, present there.*

Dr. Brown looked around the table with a smile and started by defining the climate as an intricately interwoven dynamics of the winds, oceans, glaciers, and precipitation. Any climate change would affect the seasons and all living organisms. We have seasons because of the tilted axis of the Earth. It receives differing sunlight in different places at different times, causing the seasons and allowing it to radiate excess warmth back. The behavior of oscillation between distance and nearness of the Earth to the Sun causes glowing summers and chilling winters, rejuvenating springs, pleasant autumns, and the rain in monsoons.

The whole world is blaming industrialization and the unrestricted use of fossil fuels for increasing atmospheric temperatures and the cause of climatic changes. This hypothesis is a fallacy because the Industrial Revolution started in England and subsequently extended to the rest of the world during the 20th century. But the world was experiencing erratic climatic events like floods, droughts, cloud bursts, and cyclonic spells even during the Pre-Industrialization period, which historical data corroborates.

Some people are linking the ongoing pandemic that had emanated from the COVID19 virus as fallout of climate change. But the world has seen pandemics like the Spanish Flu or Plague taking away millions of lives during the 19th and early 20th centuries. Presently, climatic disasters like floods in Europe to heat-waves in Canada, hurricanes across the USA, droughts in Africa, deluges in Asia, and wildfires in Australia have left a trail everywhere. The climate has changed from being a stable friend to an unknown entity. The financial losses and lost human lives caused by the drastic change in weather were humongous.

Hence the logic of industrialization and usage of fossil fuels given by the global community as the reason for the rise in atmospheric temperatures doesn't substantiate the recent adverse climatic events that were taking place around the world. Also, apprehensions are there that, during the next 15 years, the Amazonian green belt will face widespread deforestation due to forest fires resulting in the lesser conversion of carbon dioxide into oxygen. It may also partially contribute to a rise in atmospheric temperatures in that region. Therefore, the real reason for climate change, especially the consistent rise in global temperatures, is still unclear, though there are different theories, which need to be conclusively proven.

Dr. Brown concluded by saying that he had no conclusive logic to establish the actual reason for the climatic changes and thereby the causes of global warming, which, in his opinion, was not an economic or technological problem. It appeared to him as a political issue, driven by politicians, focusing primarily on getting reelected, or extending their terms in power. Their interest had been in getting short-term political gains rather than looking beyond five or ten years.

14

*T*he next speaker was Dr. Chang Min, who started with a brief introduction to the subjects of his expertise so that all others were on the same page and would be able to comprehend his perspective about global warming and climate change. He specifically focused on Willy.

Physics is all about modeling, finding mathematical stories, their equations that accurately reflect how nature works and allow humanity to use science as its survival instinct. Physics-based climate models have made it possible to predict the quantum and pace of global warming, including the consequences like rising sea levels, increased extreme rainfall events, and severe hurricanes decades before their occurrences. Under **Astrophysics,** the laws of physics and chemistry explain the birth, life, and death of stars, planets, galaxies, nebulae, and other unknown objects within the Universe. It also has links with Astronomy and Cosmology. The researchers use the knowledge of all these fields to understand the laws of the Universe. The experts explore how it began and evolved. Also carries on searching for life on any other planet.

Dr. Chang Min looked around, and with silent approval from all, he carried on by saying that he had *been monitoring the thermodynamic effects of radiation, which is emitted by different stars and planets, over the last few years. He had noticed some minute, but remarkable changes in the current data, when it was compared, with data deduced about a decade earlier. He had collected data from different time zones across the globe. As the earth orbits the sun, the planet gets differing sunlight at varying degrees. An extreme example has been the poles, where there are twenty-four hours of sun during the summer and twenty-four hours of darkness during the winter. He had recorded the observations to reconfirm the astonishing similarity at all the places. He had a feeling that there was a definite correlation between climate changes and the data recorded, during his observation, on positional changes of stars and planets.*

Dr. Min's apprehension was that there was some connection between the changes in thermodynamic radiation, as recorded by him, and climatic events like fast-moving wildfires in the US state of Colorado, the warmest year-end day in the UK, and Icemageddon warning in Alaska. These were examples of unprecedented climatic events because of positional changes in the planets. However, further research would be needed to come up with conclusive proof. While concluding, Dr. Min expressed his willingness to collaborate with interested persons present there to study the planetary movements for finding the actual cause of global warming and the resultant climatic changes.

By the time Dr. Min finished sharing his thoughts on climate change, it was already 8:00 pm. Willy drew the attention of all the guests to declare the break for dinner. It was a welcome break. The food was displayed nicely in a buffet-style setting under colorful canopies, a bit away from the conference zone so that no one could hear the conversations. The illumination by solar lamps was part of an action plan to cut down on using fossil fuels. The diffused illumination went very well with the ambiance of the place. The resort manager had arranged a group dance by local artists during the cocktail session, before dinner. The program continued for about 10 minutes and was a pleasant surprise to all.

While they served the cocktail and starters, five men and four women appeared in colorful attire. Another two men carried the drums and flutes. The performance began at a slow pace, and within a couple of minutes, picked up along the beats of drums and flute. It was a precise and well-rehearsed performance. The rhythm was quite soothing. After a serious discussion on global warming, it had a cooling effect on their minds and was enjoyed immensely by all of them.

15

*T*he group was back at the conference table after about 45 minutes. Bob felt that excitement was building up. All were eager to hear from Dr. Wen and Dr. Nikolova. Willy jokingly said that after food, it is tough to stay awake and apologized as he would have to adhere to the timeline. Then he requested Dr. Nikolova to go next, sharing her thoughts on the most important topic on earth. She looked up expectantly and asked everyone to address her by first name Elena.

Elena started with an analogy to explain her observations concerning global warming. She gave the example of a pan filled with boiling water and its effect on the atmosphere. When the heater is switched off, after touching the boiling point; the pan and the water start cooling down until the temperature equates with the surrounding atmosphere, as the hot water in the pan will have little influence on the outside temperature. On the contrary, the surrounding atmosphere would facilitate the cooling down of the pan and the water to match the temperature in the surrounding atmosphere. Therefore, it conclusively proves that cold weather would naturally cool down the hot air emitted from industrial units in the vicinity instead of heating the entire surrounding atmosphere. It is a natural phenomenon and is always true under any circumstances. This simple fact had been wrongly propagated to the world population by a section of people.

Now the whole world has been blaming industrialization and thereby burning fossil fuels as the cause of global warming. The temperature on Earth is varied based on the amount of radiation received by that particular area of landmass. There are large landmasses in the Arctic and Antarctic regions that are perennially covered by hardened ice due to low radiation caused by indirect sun rays. The extreme cold weather had hindered the growth of industries, making the atmosphere less polluted. Lower population density gave little scope for greenhouse gas emissions. But the melting of glaciers and the thinning of ice layers tell a different story. The recent expansive forest fire in Siberia, the coldest place on Earth, is another example of the erratic behavior of the climate.

Therefore, the melting of ice in the Antarctic region had been a natural phenomenon and not influenced by industrialization and the usage of fossil fuels. Again, the El Nino Southern Oscillation, or ENSO, is another natural phenomenon that occurred at erratic time intervals for hundreds of years from much before industrialization. The warming of the ocean across the east-central equatorial Pacific region causes significant changes to typical global atmospheric patterns. The efforts by the international *community to link the rise in atmospheric temperatures and industrialization would be a futile exercise, not leading to any feasible solution for containing the levels of warming.*

Elena continued by saying that the international community participating in the global conferences needs to understand the problem of global warming from the proper perspective before taking pledges to walk backward from civilization without the knowledge of results, only to be known after decades to the forthcoming generations. The effect known is that the atmosphere is getting warmer, but the real cause is still a gray area. Climate change is like the disease of Cancer: The causes of cancer are still under investigation by researchers. Also, there are impressions that climate change and the spread of infectious diseases are connected in more ways than they are immediately recognized. Viruses form about 15% of all known human pathogens but account for almost 50% of new and emerging diseases. Since the mid-twentieth century, about 75% of all emerging viruses were zoonotic and spilled over into humans from animals. The reasons were deforestation and climate change due to atmospheric pollution and may be due to industrialization. Melting ice caused by global warming could also unleash ancient microbes lying dormant under glaciers. The 2016 outbreak of anthrax in Siberia had led to the culling of more than two hundred thousand reindeers. Furthermore, many of the unknown viruses discovered from glacial ice cores are supposed to be thousands of years old. All those viruses contained at one point in time; are activated again and become the cause of diseases leading to a potential catastrophe.

<h1 style="text-align:center">16</h1>

*B*ob noticed that the guests were taking notes on their notepads. Until then, there was not much headway as far as the real cause of global warming was concerned, and the group was eager to hear Dr. Wen's viewpoint. He adjusted his spectacles and started by saying that the rate of changes in atmospheric temperatures is the determinant factor for warming or cooling the air. Heat absorption is highest when an object is in direct exposure to the radiation of the sun for a longer duration. If we look at the inner planets, Venus is very hot while Mars is very cold and, Earth is just right. Again, the tilt of the Earth's axis determines the solar input at different parts. The radiation is high where the daylight is for a longer duration, and accordingly, seasonal changes are taking place.

As there is no uniformity in the radiation from the sun, the proposal for the generation and transmission of solar power as a source of clean energy under the concept of **one-world-one-grid** might pose a big challenge. However, the global community had accepted the fact, though passively, that solar radiation had increased over the years and might be the reason for planning to harness it for the generation of clean energy as an alternative to the usage of fossil fuels. But it would not solve the problem. Because it is doubtful to what extent solar power may cut back on the use of fossil fuels and contribute to a reduction in atmospheric pollution. Therefore, producing alternative energy and saving the world from submerging is more a myth than a reality.

Over the years, the scientific discoveries and inventions that led to industrialization were mostly for manufacturing products to provide comfort and luxury to people. The more dangerous part of it has been the production of equipment for mass destruction in the name of national security. It also gave the pride of power and supremacy by waging wars against fellow humans. Hence, de-industrialization is not a viable option, especially from a political viewpoint.

Presently, the rich and powerful nations and a few super-rich individuals are investing billions of dollars in space exploration missions, which is encouraging and a positive step towards the survival of a small percentage of the population, though it is ephemeral. When the earth itself would not exist, the supply chain of essentials would also not exist unless they're produced sufficiently at space stations. It is being experimented successfully by growing chili at the International Space Station.

Nevertheless, in the present phase of unpredictable climatic behavior, all the shortsighted investments in *fixing climate change would get washed away. In the past 20 years, heat-related deaths have increased by around 15% in the G20 countries. The forest fires have burnt an area one and a half times the size of Canada. Climate change has impacted all aspects of life, be it food supplies, health, or ways of making a living. But the real reason for global warming and the resultant climate change is still unclear. Hence, initiating proposed actions based on incomplete information might be counter-productive.*

17

*A*ll *four guests shared their erudite thoughts on climate change and the imminent disastrous* situation that the world would probably face by the end of this millennium. There is no full-proof solution in hand. A variety of nation-specific social, economic, and political resistance towards a unified approach for dealing with this grave situation is another big challenge.

The overall situation was quite alarming. The leaders from under-developed and developing countries have geared up to take a larger slice of the global budget of a $100 billion annual grant from the rich and developed countries to implement the agreed action plan for achieving the targeted reduction in the emission of greenhouse gas. On the contrary, wealthy nations are reluctant to release the funds, which they had agreed at the conferences on global warming, though there was no binding clause, leaving the entire world in a state of impasse.

It was Bob's turn to talk on the most sought-after subject. He had spent considerable time researching the same. It was evident from the looks of all the other guests that they were anxious to hear him out, expecting that

Americans are always ahead with some new theory. He started with the laws of nature, based on logical inferences and by applying Observational Science. He began with the analogy of an egg, which signifies the point of birth.

Under natural circumstances, an egg is ready to hatch a baby bird on applying the body warmth of the mother bird. Life contained inside the egg-shell, in liquid form, transforms into a living baby bird under normal circumstances, having all the perfectly functional organs it would need for survival. As a natural phenomenon, the baby bird would grow into a full-size bird and lay more eggs to continue the propagation. On the contrary, any additional heat from an external source would transform the same egg into a lifeless object. Hence, life inside the egg-shell would die because of excess heat.

Similarly, when excess heat radiated on the planet, water from oceans, seas, rivers, and other water bodies would evaporate and transform into atmospheric moisture to form clouds and fall as rain. The glaciers and hardened ice in the northern hemisphere would also start melting due to excess radiation and flow down towards the sea. Therefore, the combined volume of flowing water from the mountains and the rainfall-induced accumulated water would flood the entire landmass. Additionally, a rise in sea levels due to the melting of glaciers and ice, especially from the Antarctic region, would submerge the coastal belts. There would not be an outlet for the floodwater to merge with the sea. This phenomenon would indicate the beginning of the destruction process.

Hypothetically, as part of a natural phenomenon, in case of excess radiation, the liquid from the earth would evaporate as moisture, and simultaneous forest fires would destroy vegetation turning the green planet into a dead one.

Furthermore, the tilted axis of the earth and its positional proximity to the sun made the summers warmer. Hence, the earth's proximity to the sun had been the cause of a consistent rise in atmospheric temperatures. Therefore, variation in solar radiation causes seasonal changes as a natural phenomenon, and it proves to have an inevitable influence on climate.

Bob stopped for a while before articulating his theory on the cause of global warming.

He started with his presumption that the actual cause of global warming had been the consequence of a contraction in the elliptical path along which the planet revolves. It had led to a reduction in the distance between Earth and the Sun. It is happening at a consistent rate over millions of years or more. The amount of solar radiation that the planet would be receiving due to further proximity in the future would increase natural events like volcanic eruptions and earthquakes. Such events would disintegrate the hard soil or rocks, which are solidified molten liquid, into smaller pieces shooting out in all directions into space due to the inertia of motion of the rotating planet. This phenomenon would reduce the size of the earth and thereby lead to its extinction from the solar system. It is a phenomenon of getting a dead one replaced by a new one as part of Universal evolution. Thus the cycle of birth and death is proven by adhering to the laws of nature.

Bob continued by saying that until then, the knowledge of the entire scientific community, put together, knew very little about the laws of nature and the universal rules. There were no such tools or technology for measuring and recording the changes in the distance between the sun and other planets around it with reliable accuracy. Thus far, what was known, had been by the process of approximation. Under these circumstances, it is impossible to ascertain any specific timeline for the eventuality.

The laws of nature follow a gradual path of Birth, Growth, Decay, and Extinction. All species would live through the same life cycle, which also applies to the entire Universe. The sporadic occurrences of climatic events in different parts of the world would continuously remind humanity about the ensuing catastrophe; until its actual annihilation.

The earth is exposed to escalating radiation as it gets closer to the sun; over a very long time scale. Hence, the increase in atmospheric temperature has direct links to orbital contraction.

The laws of nature are irreversible, and no power on earth can stop this predestined natural phenomenon of Creation or Birth, Growth or Development, Decay, and

Death or Extinction. The world had countless pieces of evidence of prehistoric creatures that had gone through the process and were extinct for a long time. The present and future generations would also encounter a similar fate. The creation and destruction have been a continuous process, similar to the sea waves breaking at the dykes.

As a consequence of proximity to the sun, natural disasters like floods, droughts, forest fires, earthquakes, cloud bursts, and cyclones due to depressions at sea would increase, leaving footprints of destruction, which would have an impact on every living organism. For millions of years, the earth went through transformations. It transformed from a fireball of molten liquid into a frozen planet. Then, to the living planet humanity is experiencing. It went through an evolution, approximately over the last two hundred thousand years of known human history. Hence, the theory of orbital contraction, or the path through which the earth revolves around the sun, holds good. However, the problem with climate change is that it exists on such a large time-scale that people have difficulty comprehending it and are in denial of this eventuality.

The theory had surprised the guests, who all possessed developed scientific brains. It never struck them the fact thatUniverse itself also had a life-cycle with an irreversible self-destructing mechanism. A few of them had partially similar observations deduced from the study of planetary radiation. It's like a stage IV cancer patient whose death is inevitable. No amount of medication or *any other treatment by the most experienced doctors in the world can change destiny.*

After giving a long lecture, Bob excused himself for a smoking break before concluding his talk. Right then, a gust of moist wind rushed from the sea with a whistling sound. Willy quickly stood up and decided to go inside, expecting the possibility of rain.

The group went in and sat around a long table inside the conference room. Bob continued with his concluding part. He mentioned that a few powerful and highly influential people were already aware of the eventuality without knowing the real cause of such erratic climatic behavior. They had already started preparations by investing hugely in space missions because it was clear that nothing would be left on earth to save their lives. The only hope would be to build space stations so that a new and habitable planet could be explored, as an alternate home, despite it being a very long-term plan and might have to be taken forward by the upcoming generations. The work on the food supply on space stations had already reached a promising stage by producing foodstuffs in laboratories, and the progress had been encouraging. One of the south-east Asian countries had already approved Lab-food for commercial production after all necessary health & safety checks.

18

Bob was about to say something when suddenly the lights went off, and the whole place became dark; at that instant, he was hit on the right side of his head and shoulder by something quite heavy, like a wooden log. Fortunately, he had his senses to realize that he was floating in the seawater. Momentarily, he was bewildered and couldn't fathom what had happened to him, as nothing was visible within sight. He could hear only the whistling sound of the wind, which was deafening. As time elapsed, he realized that it would be tough to stay afloat without any support in that raging sea. The huge waves were rising high and going low continuously. He thought about Willy and others, the resort, its Manager, and the servers. There was no trace of any of them; it appeared to him that everything had been swallowed by the sea and enveloped by darkness.

For a split second, the word "Doomsday" flashed in his mind, and as a matter of sheer coincidence, the date was also November 9th or 9/11, which he remembered.

He could not believe that Earth would get destroyed at that very moment. At the same time realized, that he was *about to die, as it would not be possible for him to fight the demonic waves for long. He tried to recollect when he last met Diana, and if Earth survives, how she would react on hearing the news of his death. He remembered her smiling face and thought that the news of his death would be heartbreaking, but she, being a strong woman, would be able to surmount the trauma over time. He felt excruciating pain in his right shoulder and head because of the injury. His limbs were also becoming numb. He could not recollect how long he had been struggling to stay afloat and thought that whether it was doomsday or not, it was probably his last day on the beautiful Earth.*

At that moment, some flat object came floating by his side, something similar to a wooden door. He raised his head towards the sky and thanked the Almighty, acknowledging his blessings, and tossed himself up on top of it, holding the plank with all his strength while being shrouded in darkness.

HONG KONG

19

*B*ob felt that a faint noise was coming and receding intermittently. He tried to move his limbs but could not because of excruciating pain on the right side, though unable to pinpoint the exact source of the pain. Again heard the sound and realized that it was a female voice. He tried to open his eyes and could see only a blurred female figure in a bent posture telling him something which didn't make any sense to him. Again there was absolute silence, and everything went dark.

The intermittent oscillation of his senses continued for some more time, and finally, he felt some sensation and then heard a female voice calling him by his first name. He tried opening his eyes. It took a few seconds for his eyes to get adjusted to the bright LED lights, but then he could see clearly and was elated by the sight of Diana sitting beside his bed wearing her signature smile. She looked straight into his eyes and kissed him on his forehead to assure him that she was there to take care of everything, and hence he need not worry.

Bob felt much better after seeing Diana beside him. He looked up at the attending nurse and asked her how *he came to that hospital, as his last recollection was that he was floating on something like a wooden plank in the middle of the ocean while desperately trying to stay afloat for survival.*

The nurse looked at Diana and requested her to share the details, as the resident doctor briefed Diana on her arrival from the US. She took the cue and told Bob that he was the only survivor found floating on a wooden plank near the Sri Lankan coast. A Chinese marine vessel rescued him and airlifted him to that hospital in Hong Kong. He had been unconscious for the last six days with a head injury and fractured right arm. The island, where they went, had been washed away, including all the guests, local people, and the Resort itself. Bob looked at Diana while wanting to erase the entire travel episode from his memory.

The attending Doctor came in to check on Bob. He was happy to see him come back to his senses. He smiled at Bob and said that his survival was nothing less than a miracle. God himself must have saved him. Hearing him, Bob smiled, remembering how he swung between life and death in the middle of the ocean. The doctor also informed that HK police would come the next day to record his statement as part of a routine procedure and requested Diana to be present there at that time.

The doctor checked all the reports and informed Diana that Bob was doing fine and all his clinical parameters were normal apart from the fractured right arm. It would remain plastered for another five weeks. However, he would have to wait for his release until the Police Department issues the No Objection Certificate.

The doctor left the cabin, and the nurse also went to her desk behind a transparent glass partition.

Bob looked through the window towards the Hong Kong skyline. The sea was visible through the gaps between tall towers. He recollected everything they had discussed during the meeting at the Maldivian Island. He was mentally upset after hearing about the demoralizing incident from Diana. He decided to keep the entire episode, which started with a picturesque sunrise in New Jersey and ended with an astounding sunset in the Maldives, unrevealed because sometimes it was better to leave some secrets as they were.

<h1 align="center">20</h1>

Bob felt very bad for Willy and thought he would be missing him back home. He was one of his few trusted friends and was very helpful when needed. He prayed for his departed soul silently and decided to inform the heartbreaking news to the family if it had not been communicated to them already from any other source.

Diana gave a comforting smile to Bob as she was happy to get him back alive from a near-death situation. She informed him of her decision to stay with him until his recovery and told him about the plan for having a surprise vacation in Lisbon while returning to the US as the incident had inflicted tremendous mental fatigue.

Bob appreciated Diana's thoughtfulness, as Lisbon had been one of his favorite places. He was fascinated by the beautiful sunny weather, great nightlife, colorful buildings, the Belem Tower, and the exotic seafood of the hilly coastal city. All of it gave a memorable experience, especially whenever Diana had been there with him.

Bob smiled at Diana and held her hand tightly in his left hand, appreciating her presence by his side at a time *when needed the most. He realized that in the past also, she was always there beside him for any support.*

They laughed together, and Bob felt that all his physical pain had vanished, but not the life on the beautiful Earth, which was very reassuring.